8

JUNIOR CLASSICS

Published in Red Turtle by
Rupa Publications India Pvt. Ltd 2016
7/16, Ansari Road, Daryaganj
New Delhi 110002

Sales centres:
Allahabad Bengaluru Chennai
Hyderabad Jaipur Kathmandu
Kolkata Mumbai

ISBN: 978-81-291-3892-7

First impression 2016

10 9 8 7 6 5 4 3 2 1

Contents

The Strange Case of Dr Jekyll and Mr Hyde

Robert Louis Stevenson

Mr Utterson, the lawyer, was a lean and a lifeless person. Yet, he was affectionate and could bear any height of tolerance.

It came easy to Mr Utterson, for he would not express any emotion, and even his friendship involved men of good nature. It is the mark of a modest man to accept his friendly circle ready-made; and that was the lawyer's way. His friends were those of his own blood or those whom he had known the longest; his affections, were the growth of time. Hence, the bond with Mr Richard Enfield, his distant cousin, the well-known man about town. Like Mr Utterson, Mr Enfield was reserved, formal and scornful of gossip; indeed, the two men often walked together for long stretches without saying a word to one another. It was reported by those who ran into them in their Sunday walks, that they said nothing, looked dull and found the comfort in each other's presence. For all that, the two men not only set aside occasions of pleasure, but even resisted the calls of business, that they might enjoy them uninterrupted.

It so happened that on one of these strolls, their way led them down a bystreet in a busy quarter of London. The street was small and quiet, but it drove a thriving trade on the weekdays. The inhabitants were all doing well.

Even on Sunday, the street shone out in contrast to its dingy neighbourhood, like a fire in a forest; and with its freshly painted shutters, well-polished brasses and general cleanliness, instantly attracted them.

Two doors from one corner, on the left hand going east, the line was broken by the entry of a court; and just at that point, a certain sinister block of building thrust forward its gable on the street. It was two storeys high; showed no window, nothing but a door on the lower storey bore the marks of negligence in every feature. The door, which was equipped with neither bell nor knocker, was blistered and distained.

When Mr Enfield and the lawyer came closer to the entry, the former lifted up his cane and pointed.

'It is connected in my mind with a very odd story.'

'Indeed,' said Mr Utterson, with a slight change of voice, 'and what was that?'

'Well, it was this way,' said Mr Enfield. 'I was coming home from some place at the end of the world, about three o'clock of a black winter morning, and my way lay through a part of town where there was literally nothing to be seen but lamps.

'All at once, I saw two figures: one a little man who was stumping along at a good pace, and the other a girl of maybe eight or ten who was running as hard as she was able down a cross street. The two ran into one another at the corner and then came the horrible part of the thing: the man trampled calmly over the child's body and left her screaming on the ground. It was hellish to see.

'I took to my heels, caught this gentleman and brought him back to where there was already a group surrounding the screaming child. He was perfectly cool and made no resistance, but gave me one look, so ugly that it brought out the sweat on me. The people who had turned out were the girl's own family; and pretty soon, the doctor, for whom she had been sent, put in his appearance.

'The gentleman was asked to shell out a hundred pounds. He took us to that door, whipped out a key, went in and returned with the matter of ten pounds in gold and a cheque for the balance.'

Mr Utterson was keen on learning about the drawer of the cheque. He lived around Cavendish Square, and was a rich and celebrated person. When he asked about the man in the door Mr Enfield said that it was best not to enquire. But he had studied the place for himself and it barely seemed like a house. There was no other door, and nobody went in or out of that one but, once in a great while, the gentleman.

'But for all that,' said Mr Utterson, 'there's one point I want to ask: I want to ask the name of that man who walked over the child.'

'Well,' said Mr Enfield, 'I can't see what harm it would do. It was a man of the name of Hyde.'

'Hmm,' said Mr Utterson. 'What sort of a man is he to see?'

'He is not easy to describe. There is something wrong with his appearance; something displeasing, something downright unpleasant.'

Mr Utterson again walked some way in silence and obviously under a weight of consideration.

'You are sure he used a key?' he enquired at last.

'My dear, sir ...' began Mr Enfield, surprised out of himself.

'Yes, I know,' said Mr Utterson, 'I know it must seem strange. The fact is, if I do not ask you the name of the other party, it is because I know it already. You see, Richard, your tale has gone home.

If you have been unsure in any point, you had better correct it.'

'I think you might have warned me,' said Mr Utterson, with a touch of sullenness. 'But I have been exact. The fellow had a key; and what's more, he has it still. I saw him use it, not a week ago.'

Mr Utterson sighed deeply, while the young man continued, 'Here is another lesson to say nothing. Let us make a bargain never to refer to this again.'

'With all my heart,' said the lawyer. 'I shake hands on that, Richard.'

That evening, MrUtterson returned to his house. After dinner, he took up a candle and went into his businessroom. There he opened his safe, took from the most private part of it a document endorsed on the envelope as Dr Jekyll's Will, and sat down to study its contents. The will was a handwritten document, for Mr Utterson, though he took charge of it now that it was made, had refused to lend the least assistance in the making of it; it provided that, in case of death of Henry Jekyll, all his possessions were to pass into the hands of his 'friend and benefactor Edward Hyde'.

The document offended him as a lawyer.

'I thought it was madness,' he said, as he replaced the paper in the safe, 'and now I begin to fear it is disgrace.'

With that he blew out his candle, put on a coat and set forth in the direction of Cavendish Square, where his friend, the great Dr Lanyon, had his house. 'If anyone knows, it will be Lanyon,' he had thought.

The butler welcomed him to the dining room where Dr Lanyon sat alone. This was a hearty, healthy, red-faced gentleman. At the sight of Mr Utterson, he sprang up from his chair and welcomed him with both hands. For these two were old friends, old mates from school and college, they thoroughly enjoyed each other's company.

After a little talk, the lawyer led up to the subject.

'I suppose, Lanyon,' said he, 'you and I must be the two oldest friends that Henry Jekyll has?'

'I wish the friends were younger,' chuckled Dr Lanyon. 'But I suppose we are. And what of that? I see little of him now.'

'Indeed?' said Mr Utterson. 'I thought you had a bond of common interest.'

'We had,' was the reply. 'But it is more than ten years since Henry Jekyll became too fanciful for me. He began to go wrong, wrong in mind.'

This little spirit of temper was somewhat of a relief to Mr Utterson.

'Did you ever come across a protégé of his—one Hyde?' he asked.

'Hyde?' repeated Dr Lanyon. 'No. Never heard of him.'

That was the amount of information that the lawyer carried back with him that night, leaving him impatient as he lay down on his bed.

Soon enough, Mr Utterson began to haunt the door in the bystreet of shops. In the morning before office hours, at noon when business was plenty, at night under the face of the fogged city moon, the lawyer was to be found on his chosen post.

And at last his patience was rewarded. It was a

fine dry night; frost in the air; the streets as clean as a ballroom floor; the lamps, unshaken, by any wind, drawing a regular pattern of light and shadow. By ten o'clock, when the shops were closed, the bystreet was very solitary and silent.

Mr Utterson had been some minutes at his post, when he was aware of an odd, light footstep drawing near.

The steps drew swiftly nearer, and swelled out suddenly louder as they turned the end of the street. The lawyer, looking forth from the entry, could soon see what manner of man he had to deal with. He was small and very plainly dressed, and the look of him, even at that distance, went somehow strongly against the watcher's inclination. But he made straight for the door, crossing the roadway to save time; and as he came, he drew a key from his pocket like one approaching home.

Mr Utterson stepped out and touched him on the shoulder as he passed.

'Mr Hyde, I think?'

Mr Hyde shrank back with a hissing intake of the breath. But his fear was only momentary though he did not look the lawyer in the face, he answered coolly enough, 'That is my name. What do you want?'

'I see you are going in,' said the lawyer. 'I am an old friend of Dr Jekyll's—Mr Utterson of Gaunt Street—you must have heard my name; and meeting you so conveniently, I thought you might admit me.'

'You will not find Dr Jekyll; he is away from home,' replied Mr Hyde, blowing in the key. And then suddenly, but still without looking up, 'How did you know me?' he asked.

'On your side,' said Mr Utterson, 'will you do me a favour?'

'With pleasure,' replied the other. 'What shall it be?'

'Will you let me see your face?' asked the lawyer.

Mr Hyde appeared to hesitate, and then, as if upon some sudden reflection, fronted about with an air of defiance, and the pair stared at each other pretty fixedly for a few seconds.

'Now I shall know you again,' said Mr Utterson. 'It may be useful.'

'Yes,' said Mr Hyde, 'it is as well we have, met, and you should have my address.'

And he gave a number of a street in Soho.

'Good God!' thought Mr Utterson, 'can he, too, have been thinking of the will?' But he kept his thoughts to himself and only grunted in acknowledgement of the address.In the next moment, with extraordinary quickness, Mr Hyde unlocked the door and disappeared into the house.

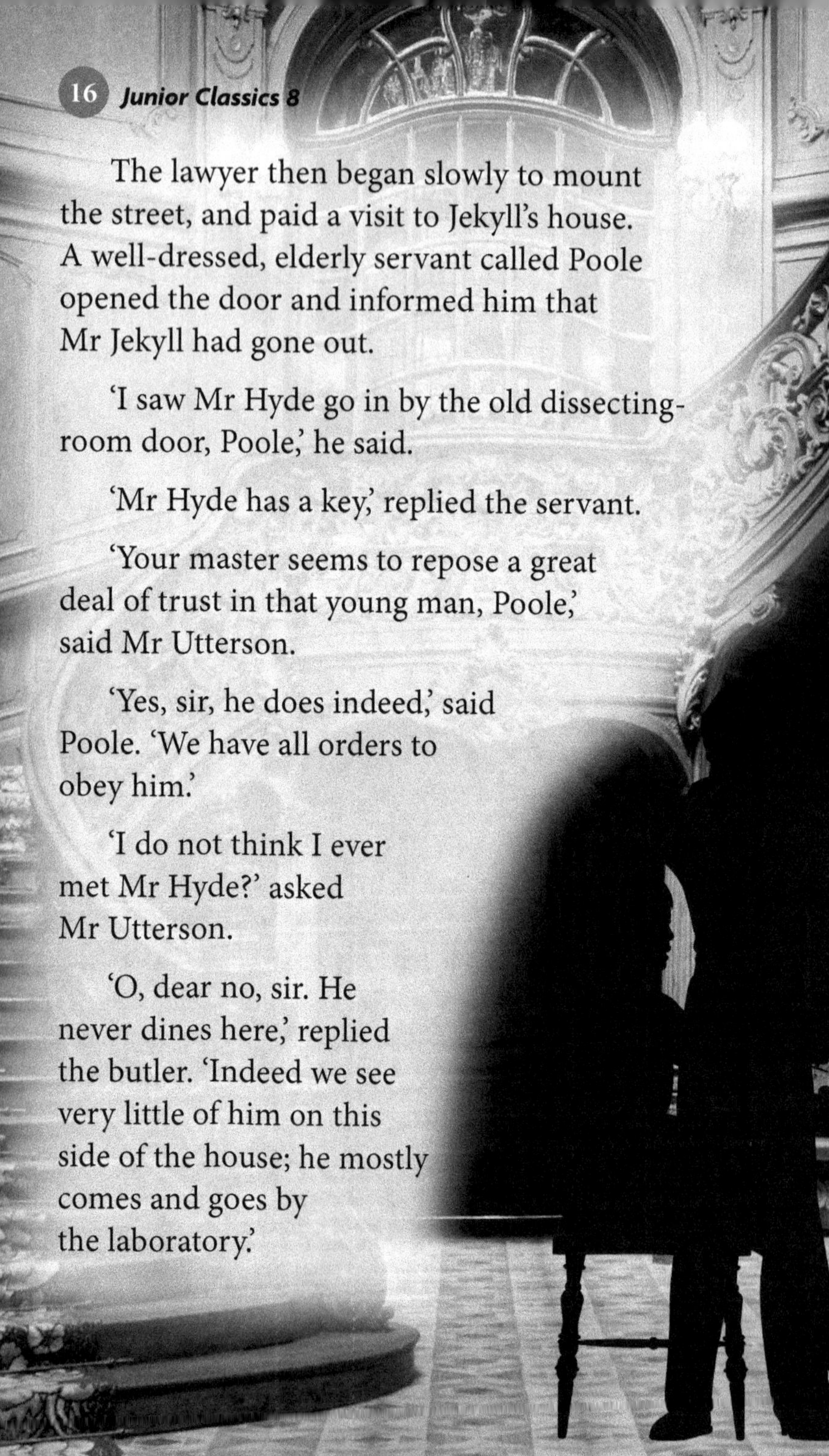

The lawyer then began slowly to mount the street, and paid a visit to Jekyll's house. A well-dressed, elderly servant called Poole opened the door and informed him that Mr Jekyll had gone out.

'I saw Mr Hyde go in by the old dissecting-room door, Poole,' he said.

'Mr Hyde has a key,' replied the servant.

'Your master seems to repose a great deal of trust in that young man, Poole,' said Mr Utterson.

'Yes, sir, he does indeed,' said Poole. 'We have all orders to obey him.'

'I do not think I ever met Mr Hyde?' asked Mr Utterson.

'O, dear no, sir. He never dines here,' replied the butler. 'Indeed we see very little of him on this side of the house; he mostly comes and goes by the laboratory.'

'Well, goodnight, Poole.'

'Goodnight, Mr Utterson.'

A fortnight later, Dr Jekyll gave one of his dinners to some five or six old cronies, all intelligent, reputable men. Towards the end of the evening, Mr Utterson remained behind after the others had departed. Where Mr Utterson was liked, he was liked well. Hosts often liked to keep Mr Utterson and enjoy his company when the others had left, and Dr Jekyll was no exception.

Mr Utterson mentioned the will to which Dr Jekyll did not want to speak. He told the lawyer firmly that everything concerning Mr Hyde was in

order and he was to be left alone. However Dr Jekyll did manage to extract a promise from Mr Utterson that he should help Mr Hyde in his absence if need be.

***

After almost a year, London was shocked by a crime of a person who held a high position in the town. A maid servant living alone in a house not far from the river, had sat down to look outside the window admiring the brilliantly lit moon. She saw an aged and handsome old gentleman, drawing near along the lane and another gentleman drawing near to meet him. She recognized the other man to be Mr Hyde, who had once visited her master and for whom she had conceived a dislike. He had in his hand a heavy cane.

Then all of a sudden he broke out in a great flame of anger, stamping with his foot, brandishing the cane like a madman. The old gentleman took a step back, with the air of one very much surprised and hurt; and at that Mr Hyde clubbed him to the earth. And next moment, with ape-like fury, he was trampling his victim under foot and hailing down a storm of blows. At the horror of the sight and sound, the maid fainted.

It was two o' clock when she came to herself and called for the police. The murderer was gone long ago, but there lay his victim in the middle of

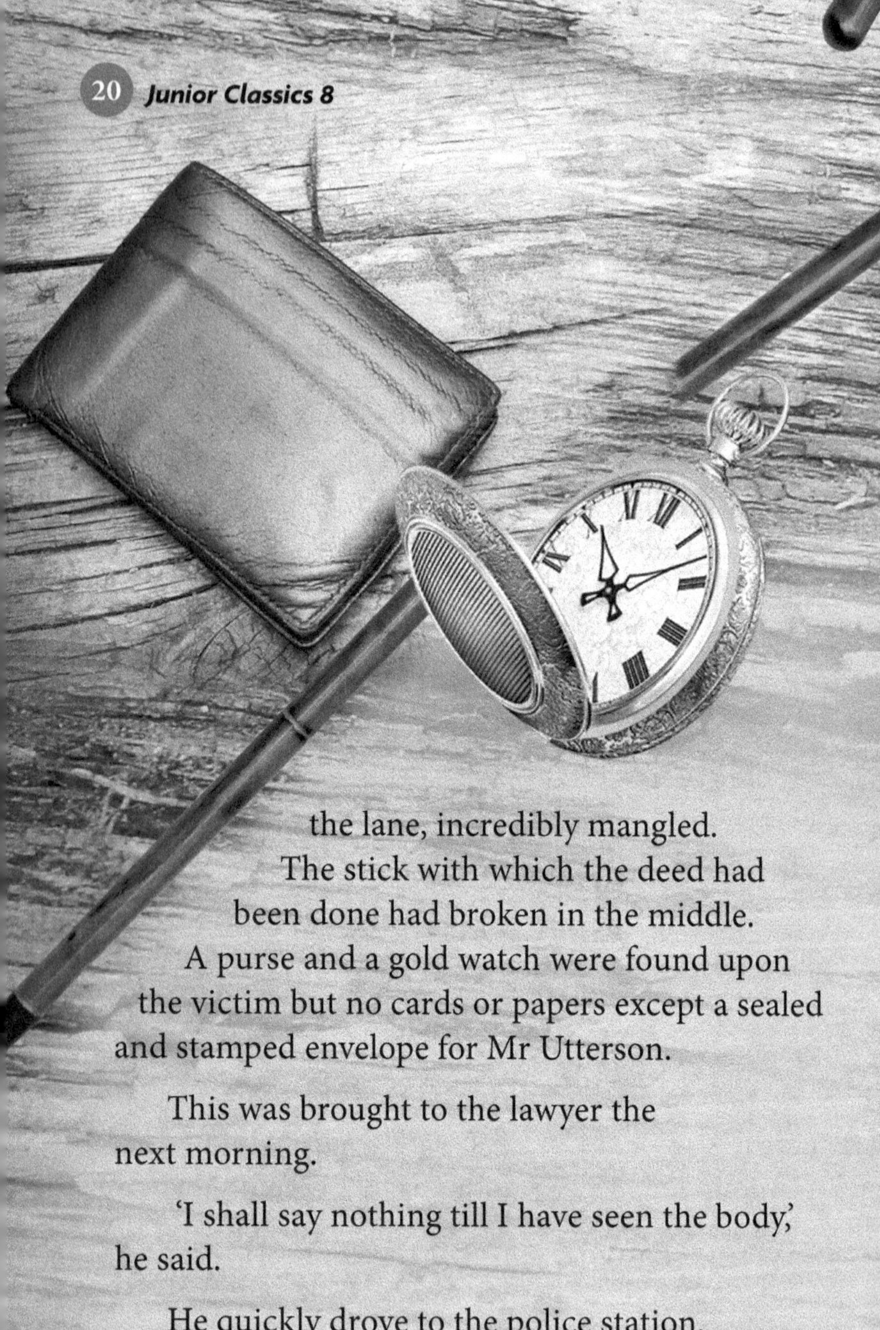

the lane, incredibly mangled. The stick with which the deed had been done had broken in the middle. A purse and a gold watch were found upon the victim but no cards or papers except a sealed and stamped envelope for Mr Utterson.

This was brought to the lawyer the next morning.

'I shall say nothing till I have seen the body,' he said.

He quickly drove to the police station.

'Yes,' said he, 'I recognize him. I am sorry to say that this is Sir Danvers Carew.'

'Good God, sir!' exclaimed the officer, 'is it possible?'

And the next moment his eyes lighted up with professional ambition.

'This will make a deal of noise,' he said. 'And perhaps you can help us to the man.'

And then he briefly narrated what the maid had seen, and showed the broken stick.

Mr Utterson shivered at the name of Hyde, but when the stick was laid before him, he could doubt no longer; broken and battered as it was, he recognized it for one that he had himself presented many years before to Henry Jekyll.

'Is this Mr Hyde a person of small stature?' he asked.

'Particularly small and particularly wicked-looking, is what the maid calls him,' said the officer.

Mr Utterson reflected; and then, raising his head, 'If you will come with me,' he said, 'I think I can take you to his house.'

A silver-haired woman opened the door and told them that Mr Hyde wasn't at home. The police searched the rooms of the house. They found the other half of the stick which strengthened their doubt about the murderer. It was claimed that Mr Utterson had gifted this stick to Dr Jekyll.

It was late in the afternoon, when Mr Utterson found his way to Dr Jekyll's door.

'And now,' said Mr Utterson, 'you have heard the news?'

The doctor shuddered.

'They were talking about it in the square,' he said.

Mr Utterson said, 'Carew was my client, but so are you, and I want to know what I am doing. You have not been mad enough to hide this fellow?'

'Utterson, I swear to God,' cried the doctor, 'I swear to God I will never set eyes on him again. I bind my honour to you that I am done with him in this world. It is all at an end. And indeed he does not want my help; you do not know him as I do; he is safe, he is quite safe; mark my words, he will never more be heard of.'

The lawyer listened gloomily; he did not like his friend's feverish manner.

'You seem pretty sure of him,' said he, 'and for your sake, I hope you may be right. If it came to a trial, your name might appear.'

'I am quite sure of him,' replied Dr Jekyll. 'I have grounds for certainty that I cannot share with anyone. But there is one thing on which you may advise me. I have—I have received a letter and I am at a loss whether I should show it to the police. I should like to leave it in your hands, Utterson; you would judge wisely, I am sure; I have so great a trust in you.'

'You fear, I suppose, that it might lead to his detection?' asked the lawyer.

'No,' said the other. 'I cannot say that I care what becomes of Hyde; I am quite done with him. I was thinking of my own character, which this hateful business has rather exposed.'

'Well,' said he, at last, 'let me see the letter.'

The letter was written in an odd, upright hand and signed 'Edward Hyde', and it signified, briefly enough, that the writer's benefactor, Dr Jekyll, whom he had long so unworthily repaid for a thousand generosities, need not worry about his safety, as he had means of escape on which he placed a sure dependence. The lawyer liked this letter well enough; it put a better colour on the intimacy than he had looked for, and he blamed himself for some of his past suspicions.

On his way out, the lawyer stopped and had a word or two with Poole who assured him that all post had come as part of daily mail and no person exceptionally had come to deliver any post.

Later when Mr Utterson sat down to discuss the letter with Mr Guest, his head clerk, he was told that the writing was that of Dr Jekyll himself.

Time ran on; thousands of pounds were offered in reward, but Mr Hyde was nowhere to be traced. On the 8th of January Mr Utterson had dined at the doctor's with a small party; Dr Lanyon had been there too. On the 12th, and again on the 14th, the door was shut against the lawyer.

'The doctor was confined to the house,' Poole said, 'and saw no one.'

On the 15th, he tried again, and was again refused; and having now been used for the last two months to see his friend almost daily, he found this return of solitude to weigh upon his spirits. The fifth night he had a guest to dine with him; and the sixth he visited Dr Lanyon's place.

Dr Lanyon handed over a letter with some information related to Dr Jekyll and asked him to open it only on the death of Dr Jekyll or if he disappeared. In the following two weeks Dr Lanyon died suddenly.

Mr Utterson was sitting by his fireside one evening after dinner, when he was surprised to receive a visit from Poole. He requested the lawyer to come over to his master's house immediately as there was something serious, and they left soon in the cold March night.

'Well, sir,' Poole said, 'here we are, and God grant there be nothing wrong.'

'Amen, Poole,' said the lawyer.

Thereupon the servant knocked in a very guarded manner; the door was opened on the chain and a voice asked from within, 'Is that you, Poole?'

'It's all right,' said Poole. 'Open the door.'

The hall, when they entered it, was brightly lighted up; and filled with servants who stood huddled together like a flock of sheep.

'What, what? Why are you all here?' said the lawyer peevishly. 'Very irregular, very unseemly; your master would be far from pleased.'

'They're all afraid,' said Poole.

'Now, sir,' said he, 'you come as gently as you can. I want you to hear, and I don't want you to be heard. And see here, sir, if by any chance he was to ask you in, don't go.'

Mr Utterson followed the butler into the laboratory building.

'Mr Utterson, sir, asking to see you,' Poole called knocking on the door; even as he did so, once more violently signalled to the lawyer to give ear.

A voice answered from within, 'Tell him I cannot see anyone.'

'Thank you, sir,' said Poole, with a note of something like triumph in his voice; and taking up his candle, he led Mr Utterson back across the yard and into the great kitchen, where the fire was out.

'Sir,' he said, 'was that my master's voice?'

'It seems much changed,' replied the lawyer, very pale, but giving look for look.

'Changed? Well, yes, I think so,' said the butler. 'Have I been twenty years in this man's house, to be deceived about his voice? No, sir; master's made away with; he was made, away with eight days ago, when we heard him cry out upon the name of God; and who's in there instead of him, and why it stays there, is a thing that cries to Heaven, Mr Utterson!'

'This is a very strange tale, Poole; this is rather a wild tale, my man,' said Mr Utterson, biting his finger. 'Suppose it were as you suppose, supposing Dr Jekyll to have been—well, murdered, what could induce the murderer to stay? That won't hold water; it doesn't commend itself to reason.'

'Well, Mr Utterson, you are a hard man to satisfy, but I'll do it,' said Poole. 'All this last week (you must know) him, or it, or whatever it is that lives in that cabinet, has been crying night and day for some sort of medicine and cannot get it to his mind. It was sometimes his way—the master's, that is—to write his orders on a sheet of paper and throw it on the stair. We've had nothing else this week back; nothing but papers, and a closed door, and the very meals left there to be smuggled in when nobody was looking. Well, sir, every day, and twice and thrice in the same day, there have been orders and complaints, and I have been sent flying to all the wholesale chemists in town. Every time I brought the stuff back, there would be another paper telling me to return it because it was not pure, and another order to a different firm. This drug is wanted bitter bad, sir, whatever for.'

'Do you have you any of these papers?' asked Mr Utterson.

Poole felt in his pocket and handed out a crumpled note, which the lawyer, bending nearer to the candle, carefully examined. Its contents ran thus: 'Dr Jekyll presents his compliments to Messrs Maw. He assures them that their last sample is impure and quite useless for his present purpose. In the year 18—, Dr J. purchased a somewhat large quantity from Messrs M. He now begs them to search with utmost care, and should any of the same quality be left, to forward it to him at once. Expense is no consideration. The importance of this to Dr J. can hardly be exaggerated.'

So far the letter had run composedly enough, but here with a sudden splutter of the pen, the writer's emotion had broken loose. 'For God's sake,' he had added, 'find me some of the old.'

After this strange note, Mr Utterson realized the growing fear amongst the servants at Dr Jekyll's place, especially the voices they could hear from outside the laboratory were not normal. Even the sound of the footsteps for that matter changed, and was lighter. After a few arguments, they decided to break in to the laboratory.

It was shocking to see Mr Hyde's body lying dead in Jekyll's clothes. He had committed suicide. There also was a letter from Dr Jekyll to the lawyer revealing the mystery.

MY DEAR UTTERSON,

When this shall fall into your hands, I shall have disappeared, under what circumstances I have not the penetration to foresee, but my instinct and all the circumstances of my nameless situation tell me that the end is sure and must be early. Go then, and first read the narrative which Lanyon warned me he was to place in your hands; and if you care to hear more, turn to the confession of

Your unworthy and unhappy friend,

HENRY JEKYLL

Mr Utterson returned home and first read Dr Lanyon's letter.

10 December, 18—

DEAR LANYON,

You are one of my oldest friends; and although we may have differed at times on scientific questions, I cannot remember, at least on my side, any break in our affection. Lanyon, my life, my honour, my reason, are all at your mercy; if you fail me tonight I am lost. You might suppose, after this, that I am going to ask you for something dishonourable to grant. Judge for yourself.

I want you to postpone all other engagements for tonight—even if you were summoned to the bedside of an emperor; to take a cab and to drive straight to my house. Poole, my butler, has his orders; you will find, him waiting your arrival with a locksmith. The door of my cabinet is then to be forced: and you are to go in alone; to draw out, with all its contents as they stand, the fourth drawer from the top or the third from the bottom. In my extreme distress of wind, I have a fear of misdirecting you; but even if I am in error, you may know the right drawer by its contents: some powders, a phial and a paper book. This drawer I beg of you to carry back with you to Cavendish Square exactly as it stands.

That is the first part of the service: now for the second. At midnight, I have to ask you to be alone in your consulting room to admit with your own hand into the house a man who will present himself in my name. You have to place in his hands the drawer that you will have brought with you from my cabinet. Then you will have played your part and earned my gratitude completely.

Confident as I am that you will not trifle with this appeal, my heart sinks and my hand trembles at the bare thought of such a possibility. Think of me at this hour, in a strange place, labouring under a blackness of distress, and yet well aware that, if you will but punctually serve me, my troubles will roll away like a story that is told. Serve me, my dear Lanyon, and save

Your friend,

H. J.

P. S. I had already sealed this up when a fresh terror struck upon my soul. It is possible that the post office may fail me, and this letter not come into your hands until tomorrow morning. In that case, dear Lanyon, do my errand when it shall be most convenient for you in the course of the day; and once more expect my messenger at midnight. It may then already be too late; and if that night passes without event, you will know that you have seen the last of Henry Jekyll.

On trying to understand the contents tying loose strings together, the letter explained how Dr Lanyon took to bed and died from shock when he saw Mr Hyde drinking a potion and turning into Dr Jekyll.

The letter from Dr Jekyll unfolds the mystery. Dr Jekyll described his desire to his good-natured personality separate from that which was evil and free of conscience. This was a periodical change and was not complete by itself. He used a serum or a potion for the change in his personality, but at times he discovered that the change occurred naturally.

Sir Danvers Carew's murder was a result of one of the evil urges that gripped him to commit the crime. Eventually, the potion began to run out, and Dr Jekyll was unable to find a key ingredient to make more. His ability to change back from Mr Hyde into Dr Jekyll slowly vanished. Dr Jekyll wondered if Mr Hyde will face execution for his crimes or choose to kill himself. As the police was chasing him for the murder, Dr Jekyll trapped with helplessness locked himself in the laboratory.

When he was convinced he wouldn't be able to change himself from Mr Hyde to Dr Jekyll, he decided to write this letter of which the last lines read …

'Here then, as I lay down the pen and proceed to seal up my confession, I bring the life of that unhappy Henry Jekyll to an end.'

FRANKENSTEIN

Mary Shelley

August 5, 17—

To Mrs Saville, England

So strange an accident has happened to us that I cannot forbear recording it, although it is very probable that you will see me before these papers can come into your possession.

Last Monday (July 31st) we were nearly surrounded by ice, which closed in the ship on all sides, scarcely leaving her the sea-room which she floated. Our situation was somewhat dangerous, especially as we were compassed round by a very thick fog. We accordingly lay to, hoping that some change would take place in the atmosphere and weather. When the ship became iced in, the crew witnessed a large man in the distance riding a dogsled across the frozen ocean. Sometime later, Frankenstein appeared and we brought him aboard the ship. Frankenstein, sick and weakened by the cold, stayed on the ship while I nursed him. Frankenstein seemed broken by grief and interested only in the giant man who travelled past the ship.

Frankenstein has gradually improved health but is very silent and appears uneasy when anyone except me enters his cabin. Yet his manners are so gentle that the sailors are all interested in him, although they have had very little communication with him. For my own part, I begin to love him as a brother, and his constant and deep grief fills me with sympathy and compassion. He must have been a noble creature in his better days, being even now in wreck so attractive and amiable. I said in one of my letters, my dear Margaret that I should find no friend on the wide ocean; yet I have found a man who, before his spirit had been broken by misery, I should have been happy to have possessed as the brother of my heart.

I shall continue my journal concerning Frankenstein at intervals, should I have any fresh incidents to record.

August 13, 17—

My affection for my guest increases every day. I explained Frankenstein my desire to see and explore the North Pole at any cost, even the cost of human life. Frankenstein seemed dismayed to hear of my reckless ambition which saddened him so much that I dropped the subject.

He asked me the history of my earlier years. The tale was quickly told, but it awakened various trains of reflection. I spoke of my desire of finding a friend, of my thirst for a more intimate sympathy with a fellow who had ever fallen to my lot, and expressed my conviction that a man could boast of little happiness who did not enjoy this blessing.

'I agree with you,' replied the Frankenstein, 'we are unfashioned creatures, but half made up, if one wiser, better, dearer than ourselves—such a friend ought to be. I once had a friend, the most noble of human creatures, and am entitled, therefore, to judge respecting friendship. You have hope, and the world before you, and have no cause for despair. But I—I have lost everything and cannot begin life anew.'

As he said this his face became expressive of a calm, settled grief that touched me to the heart. But he was silent and presently retired to his cabin.

August 19, 17—

Yesterday, Frankenstein said to me, 'You may easily perceive, Captain Walton, that I have suffered great and unparalleled misfortunes. I had determined at one time that the memory of these evils should die with me, but you have won me to alter my determination. You seek for knowledge and wisdom, as I once did; and I ardently hope that the gratification of your wishes may not be a serpent to sting you, as mine has been. I do not know that the relation of my disasters will be useful to you; yet, when I reflect that you are pursuing the same course, exposing yourself to the same dangers which have rendered me what I am, I imagine that you may deduce an apt moral from my tale, one that may direct you if you succeed in your undertaking and console you in case of failure.'

Frankenstein decides to tell me his story with a hope that I can learn some lesson from the mistakes that have led to Frankenstein's ruin.

R. Walton

Frankenstein's Story

I was born in Geneva, and my family is one of the most distinguished families of that republic. My father's name was Alphonse Frankenstein, who was a wealthy, respected and benevolent man who rescued my mother, Caroline, from poverty before marrying her.

On a walk through the Italian countryside where Caroline visited the poor, she found a beautiful orphan girl being raised by a peasant family. Elizabeth Lavenza, the fair-haired, lovely orphan child, was adopted by the Frankenstein family, and I considered it my job to care of her. Elizabeth and I became inseparable from that moment.

We were brought up together; there was not quite a year difference in our ages. On the birth of their second son, younger by seven years than me, my parents gave up entirely their wandering life and fixed themselves in their native country. We possessed a house in Geneva. I attached myself intensely to only a few people, and Elizabeth and

Henry Clerval, a schoolmate, were my closest friends. Henry Clerval was the son of a merchant of Geneva. He was a boy of singular talent and limitless fancy. He loved enterprise, hardship and even danger for its own sake.

When I had attained the age of seventeen my parents resolved that I should become a student at the university of Ingolstadt. I had attended the schools of Geneva, but my father thought it necessary for the completion of my education that I should be made acquainted with other customs than those of my native country. My departure was therefore fixed at an early date, but before the day resolved upon could arrive, the first misfortune of my life occurred—an omen, as it were, of my future misery. Elizabeth got scarlet fever. As she was recovering, my mother, who had been nursing Elizabeth, fell ill. On her deathbed, she told me and Elizabeth that she wanted us to marry.

She died calmly. During the grieving period, Elizabeth was a great comfort despite her own sadness, I soon left for Ingolstadt. Henry wanted to go with me, but my father wouldn't allow it.

I was nervous about being alone and away from everyone I knew and loved, but once there, I found my seat within the science department. Partly from curiosity and partly from idleness, I went into the lecturing room, which M. Waldman entered shortly after. This professor was very unlike his colleagues. He appeared about fifty years of age, but with an aspect expressive of the greatest benevolence; a few grey hairs covered his temples, but those at the back of his head were nearly black. He began his lecture by a recapitulation of the history of chemistry and the various improvements made by different men of learning, pronouncing with fervour the names of the most distinguished discoverers. His lectures revived my interest in discovering the spark of life and creation.

I became an ardent student of chemistry and anatomy in my quest to determine what gives life.

After two years of study at Ingolstadt, I considered returning home better because my studies were so advanced that I couldn't progress any further at the college. But before I planned my trip home, I discovered the essence of life, which I refuse to reveal to you because I don't want you to follow my poor example.

I worked secretly and without rest for almost a year, during which time my correspondence with my family and friends stopped. My health began to decline from the constant labour, little rest, poor diet and lack of exercise. Winter, spring and summer passed away during my labours, but I did not watch the blossom or the expanding leaves.

It was on a dreary night of November that I beheld the accomplishment of my toils. With an anxiety that almost amounted to agony, I collected the instruments of life around me that I might infuse a spark of being into the lifeless thing that lay at my feet. It was already one in the morning; the rain pattered dismally against the panes, and my candle was nearly burnt out, when, by the glimmer of the half-extinguished light, I saw the dull yellow eye of the creature open; it breathed hard, and a convulsive motion agitated its limbs.

How can I describe my emotions at this catastrophe? His limbs were in proportion, and I had selected his features rather beautiful. Beautiful! Great God! His pale skin scarcely covered the work of muscles and arteries beneath; his hair was of a lustrous black, and flowing; his teeth of a pearly whiteness but these luxuriances only formed a more horrid contrast with his watery eyes, that seemed almost of the same colour as the white sockets in which they were set, his wrinkled complexion and straight black lips.

I had worked hard for nearly two years, for the sole purpose of infusing life into an inanimate body. For this I had deprived myself of rest and health. I had desired it with an ardour that far exceeded moderation; but now that I had finished, the beauty of the dream vanished, and breathless horror and disgust filled my heart. I fled my laboratory and collapsed in my room.

I woke from my sleep with horror; I suddenly saw the miserable monster that I had created. He held up the curtain of the bed; and his eyes, were fixed on me. His jaws opened, and he might have spoken, but I did not hear; one hand was stretched out, seemingly to detain me, but I escaped and rushed downstairs.

I ran away out into the city and walked until dawn. I ran into Henry in the city. I was so excited to see my friend that I forgot about the monster. We talked very long. I asked him about his family and he answered that all were good. When, we returned at our college, I then reflected, and the thought made me shiver, that the creature that I had left in my apartment might still be there, alive and walking about. I dreaded to see this monster, but I feared still more that Henry should see him. Entreating him, therefore, to remain a few minutes at the bottom of the stairs, I darted up towards my own room. When I opened the door fearfully, the creature was not there. The creature was gone, and I was relieved, I clapped my hands for joy and ran down to Henry but I fell down in a fit. This was the commencement of a nervous fever which confined me for several months. During all that time Henry was my only nurse. By very slow degrees, and with frequent relapses that alarmed and grieved my friend, I recovered.

One day, I found the following letter from my father:

My dear Victor,

You have probably waited impatiently for a letter to fix the date of your return to us; and I was at first tempted to write only a few lines, merely mentioning the day on which I should expect you. But that would be a cruel kindness, and I dare not do it. What would be your surprise, my son, when you expected a happy and glad welcome, to behold, on the contrary, tears and wretchedness? And how, Victor, can I relate our misfortune? Absence cannot have rendered you callous to our joys and griefs; and how shall I inflict pain on my long absent son? I wish to prepare you for the woeful news, but I know it is impossible; even now your eye skims over the page to seek the words which are to convey to you the horrible tidings.

Your small brother (William) has been murdered.

Last Thursday (May 7), I, my niece, and your two brothers were walking in the woods near our Geneva home. William and Ernest were playing. William had run away to hide himself and disappeared. About five in the morning I discovered my lovely boy, whom the night before I had seen blooming and active in health, stretched on the grass motionless; the print of the murderer's finger was on his neck. Elizabeth was distressed because she had loaned the boy a miniature, or locket of Caroline, William's dead mother, and it was no longer around his neck. The locket seemed the motive for the boy's murder, and Elizabeth felt responsible.

Come, Victor; not brooding thoughts of vengeance against the assassin, but with feelings of peace and gentleness, that will heal, instead of festering, the wounds of our minds. Enter the house of mourning, my friend, but with kindness and affection for those who love you, and not with hatred for your enemies.

Your affectionate and afflicted father,

Alphonse Frankenstein.

Geneva

May 12, 17—.

I left for Geneva immediately to comfort and grieve with my family. Returning to my hometown after six years made me nervous and afraid of the changes that had taken place there.

I clasped my hands, and exclaimed aloud, "William, dear angel!" As I said these words, I perceived in the gloom a figure hidden behind a clump of trees near me. I stood fixed, gazing intently so that I could not be mistaken. A flash of lightning illuminated the object, and discovered its shape plainly to me; its gigantic stature, and the deformity of its aspect more hideous than reality belongs to humanity, instantly informed me that it was the wretch, the filthy demon, to whom I had given life. What was he doing there? Could he be (I shuddered at the conception) the murderer of my brother? No sooner did that idea cross my imagination, than I became convinced of its truth; my teeth chattered, and I was forced to lean against a tree for support. The figure passed me quickly, and I lost it in the gloom.

Nothing in human shape could have destroyed the fair child. He was the murderer! I could not doubt it. I myself was William's murderer because I created the beast that killed him. I realized that I couldn't tell anyone that the monster murdered William because no one would believe me.

William's nanny, Justine, was to be hanged as his locket was found in her pocket.

I was full of guilt. And I had to do everything to save Justine. This state of mind preyed upon my health.

Our house was the house of mourning. My father's health was deeply shaken by the horror of the recent events. Elizabeth was sad and desponding; she no longer took delight in her ordinary occupations. My family and friends couldn't ease my mind because they didn't know the source of my trouble. They had no idea about the monster, and I couldn't tell them, I had to handle my grief alone. Sometimes I could cope with the sullen despair that overwhelmed me, but sometimes the whirlwind passions of my soul drove me to seek a change of place. One day I suddenly left my home. My wanderings were directed towards the valley of Chamounix. I had visited it frequently during my boyhood. Six years had passed since then.

I spent the following day roaming through the valley. I stood beside the sources of the Arveiron, which took their rise in a glacier that with slow pace is advancing down from the summit of the hills to barricade the valley.

I suddenly beheld the figure of a man, at some distance, advancing towards me with superhuman speed.

The monster told me that as his creator, I owed it to him to hear his story and meet his demands. If I would meet the demands, the monster vowed to withdraw from humanity and leave me in peace. If

I refused his offer he would destroy my family. Out of compassion and even greater curiosity, I agreed to listen and accompanied the monster to his ice cave in the mountains. He thus began his tale.

The monster is now intelligent and well-versed in language. He said he learnt through listening to others and gradually became a good communicator. Even then, he had to hide in the woods for people would fear his presence. He was himself shattered by his looks, while seeing his reflection in the pool. While he was staying closer to the family, the family refused to accept him, and in a fit of rage he chose to burn their cottage.

The monster further demanded that if I wanted to see him disappear, I will have to create a female companion for him.

"You must create a female for me with whom I can live. This you alone can do and you must not refuse to concede."

"I do refuse it," I replied, "and no torture shall ever make me agree to this. Shall I create another like yourself, whose joint wickedness might finish the world?"

"You are in the wrong," replied the beast, "and instead of threatening, I am content to reason with you. I am malicious because I am miserable. Am I not shunned and hated by all mankind? You, my creator, would tear me to pieces and triumph; remember that, and tell me why I should pity man more than he pities me? Let him live with me in the interchange of kindness, and instead of injury I would bestow every benefit upon him with tears of gratitude at his acceptance.

"This passion is detrimental to me, for you do not reflect that you are the cause of its excess. If any being felt emotions of benevolence towards me, I should return them a hundred and a hundredfold; for that one creature's sake I would make peace with the whole kind! But I now indulge in dreams of bliss that cannot be realized. What I ask of you is to be reasonable and moderate; I demand a creature

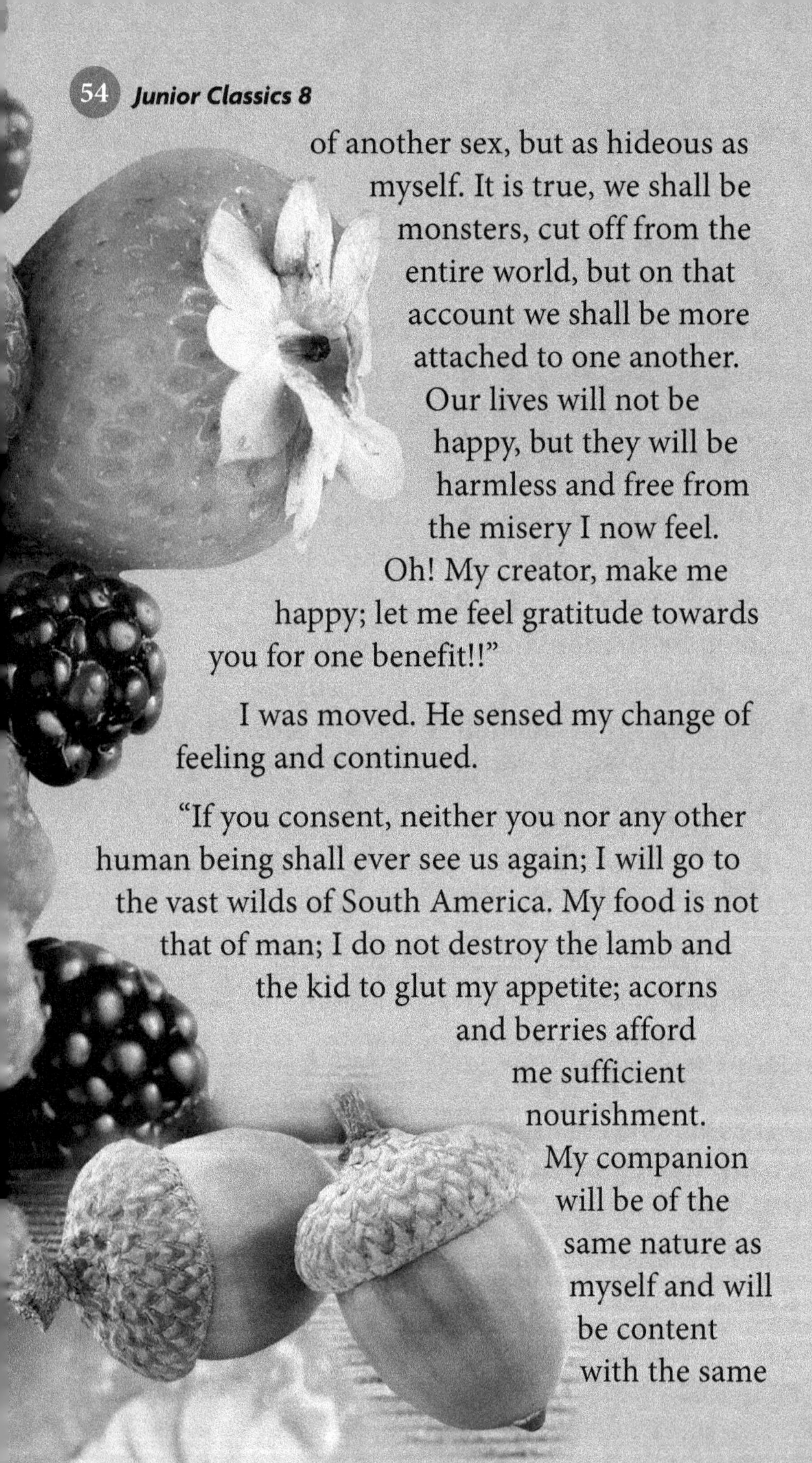

of another sex, but as hideous as myself. It is true, we shall be monsters, cut off from the entire world, but on that account we shall be more attached to one another. Our lives will not be happy, but they will be harmless and free from the misery I now feel. Oh! My creator, make me happy; let me feel gratitude towards you for one benefit!!"

I was moved. He sensed my change of feeling and continued.

"If you consent, neither you nor any other human being shall ever see us again; I will go to the vast wilds of South America. My food is not that of man; I do not destroy the lamb and the kid to glut my appetite; acorns and berries afford me sufficient nourishment. My companion will be of the same nature as myself and will be content with the same fare. We shall make our bed of dried leaves; the sun will shine on us as on man and will ripen our food. The picture I present to you is peaceful and human, and you must feel that you could deny it only in the wantonness of power and cruelty. Pitiless as you have been towards me, I now see compassion in your eyes; let me seize the favourable moment and persuade you to promise what I so ardently desire."

To protect my family of anymore trouble, I began working on his demand. I was almost finished with the female monster, but I realized that this monster might not be agreeable to all the conditions. She would be as independent as the first monster and might not be held at peace by an agreement made before her creation. She might be violent. She and the monster might procreate and introduce a race of monsters to the earth. There were so many horrific possibilities that I didn't want that responsibility.

While I was deciding against finishing the second creature, the monster looked in the window of the laboratory. Seeing the terrifying results of my first creation, I defiantly ripped the second creature apart and left the lab for my home.

Several hours passed and wretch appeared and threatened me to be with me on my wedding night.

Soon after I left for France. One day I got a letter from Elizabeth explaining that although she

wanted to marry me, she didn't want me to feel honour-bound to marry her if there was someone else whom I loved. I loved no one, but the monster had promised to be with me on my wedding night. I decided to face my death bravely and wrote to Elizabeth that I would marry her as soon as I returned and would tell her the secret that had been bothering me for so long on the day after the wedding. I returned home and was still depressed. The wedding date was set for ten days later and in the meantime, I carried a gun and dagger in case the monster showed up early. But I wasn't prepared for what the monster had in store.

In the meantime, Clerval was murdered and I ended up being the prime suspect, but I was released in a few days.

My anger knew no bounds as the monster soon confessed to the crime. But I first decided to marry Elizabeth and then chase him. As the monster had promised to be present on the first night, I left Elizabeth in the room and set off to look for him. By the time I returned Elizabeth was strangled to death.

From the window, I saw the monster taunting me of having done what he promised. My father soon died of grief after losing four members in the family.

I did everything possible I could to chase the monster at North Pole, but could not kill him.

***

Frankenstein dies shortly thereafter. Walton discovers the creature on his ship, mourning over Frankenstein's body.

Walton hears the creature's misguided reasons for his vengeance and expressions of remorse.

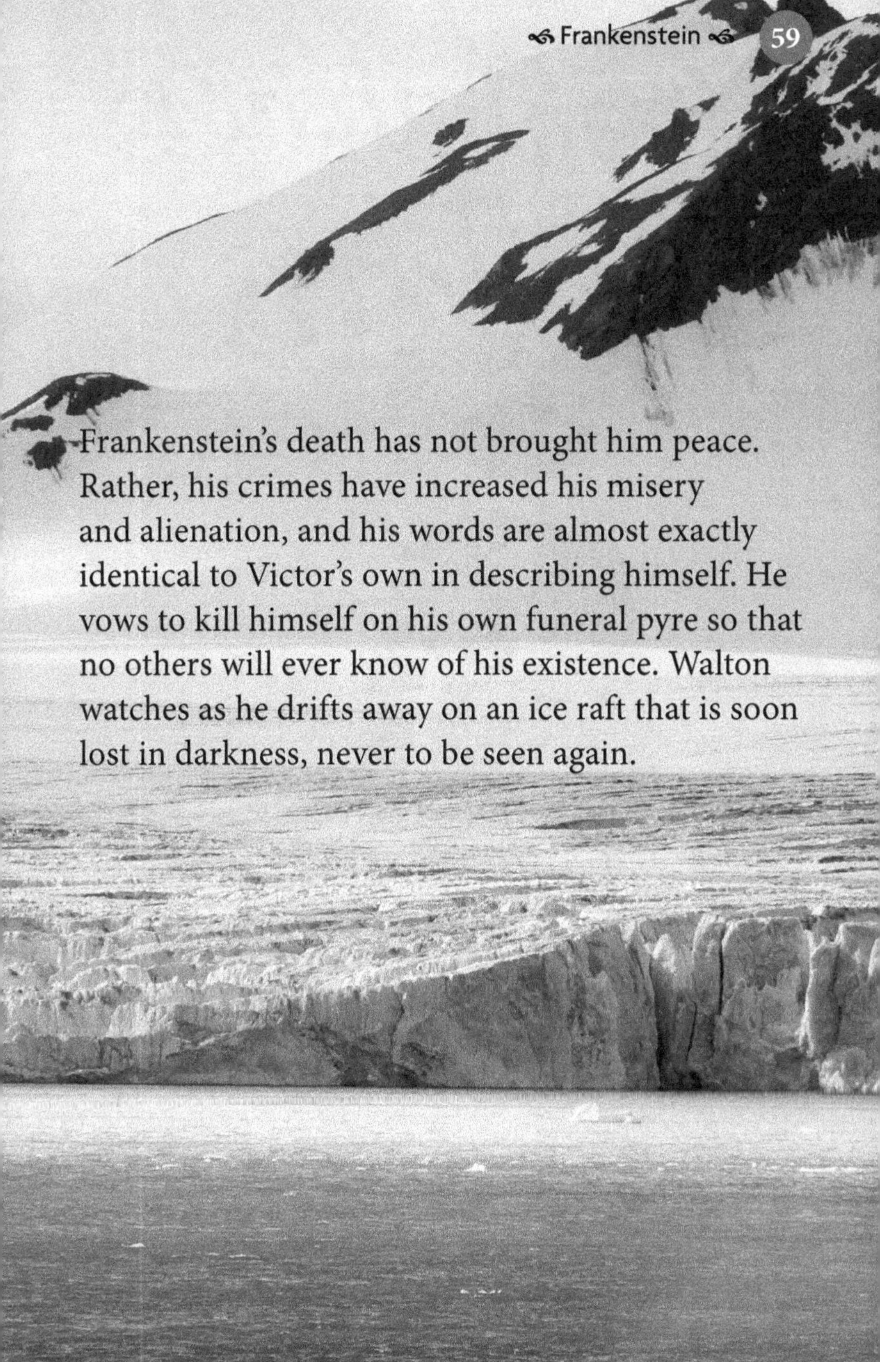

Frankenstein's death has not brought him peace. Rather, his crimes have increased his misery and alienation, and his words are almost exactly identical to Victor's own in describing himself. He vows to kill himself on his own funeral pyre so that no others will ever know of his existence. Walton watches as he drifts away on an ice raft that is soon lost in darkness, never to be seen again.

The Invisible Man

H. G. Wells

The stranger came early in February, one wintry day, through a biting wind and a driving snow. He walked from the Bamblehurst railway station, carrying a large leather travel bag. He was wrapped up from head to foot, and the brim of his soft felt hat hid every inch of his face except the shiny tip of his nose. He arrived at an inn, Coach and Horses, and said, 'A fire, in the name of human charity! A room and a fire!'

1

Mrs Hall lit the fire and left him there. She went to prepare him a meal with her own hands. A guest to stop at Iping during winter was unheard of. Although the fire was burning up briskly, she was surprised to see that her visitor still wore his hat and coat, standing with his back to her and staring out of the window at the falling snow in the yard. His gloved hands were clasped behind him, and he seemed to be lost in thought. She noticed that the melting snow that still sprinkled his shoulders dripped upon her carpet.

'Can I take your hat and coat, sir?' she said. 'And give them a good dry in the kitchen?'

'No,' he said without turning.

'Very well, sir,' she said. 'As you like. In a bit the room will be warmer.'

He made no answer, and had turned his face away from her again.

Mrs Hall, feeling that her conversational advances were ill-timed, whisked out of the room.

When she returned he was still standing there, she put down the eggs and bacon with considerable emphasis, and said to him, 'Your lunch is served, sir.'

'Thank you,' he said at the same time. Then he swung round and approached the table.

Mrs Hall went to dry his clothes and her visitor said in a muffled voice that the hat should be left there. She turned and saw that he had raised his head and looked at her while he sat there. For a moment she stood gaping at him, too surprised to speak.

He held a white cloth over the lower part of his face, so that his mouth and jaws were completely hidden due to which he had a muffled voice. But it was not that which startled Mrs Hall. It was the fact that his forehead above his blue glasses and even his ears were covered by a white bandage but his nose could be seen. It was bright, pink, and shiny just as it had been at first. He wore a dark brown velvet jacket with a high, black, linen-lined collar turned up about his neck. The thick black hair escaped as it blew between the cross bandages, projected in curious tails and horns and gave him the strangest appearance. This muffled and bandaged head was so unlike what she had anticipated that for a moment she was rigid.

'Thank you,' he said drily, glancing from her to the door and then at her again.

'I'll have them nicely dried, sir, at once,' she said, and carried his clothes out of the room.

Next day his luggage arrived through the slush. There were a couple of trunks indeed, in addition there were a box of books, and a dozen or more crates, boxes and cases, containing objects packed in straw, which seemed like glass bottles.

Many people in the town found him unusual. Perhaps the beauty of small towns is that there is gossip about one and all, especially while we are talking of Southern England. In such case the stranger displayed much more in appearance and action that he had to shine as the talk of the town.

Cuss, the doctor, was devoured by curiosity. The bandages excited his professional interest, the report of the thousand and one bottles aroused his jealous regard. All through April and May he looked for an opportunity of talking to the stranger. He was surprised to find that Mr Hall did not know his guest's name.

One day Cuss rapped at the parlour door and entered.

'Pardon my intrusion,' said Cuss to Mrs Hall.

Then the door closed and cut off Mrs Hall from the rest of the conversation. She could hear the murmur of voices for the next ten minutes, then a cry of surprise, stirring of feet and a chair flung aside, a bark of laughter, quick steps to the door and Cuss appeared his face white, his eyes staring over his shoulder. He left open the door behind him and without a look at her, strode across the hall.

Cuss went straight up the village to Bunting the vicar.

'Am I mad?' Cuss began abruptly, as he entered the shabby little study.

'What's happened?' asked the vicar.

'That chap at the inn—'

Cuss was very angry. He asked for a drink and sat down there. When his nerves had been steadied by a drink he told him of the encounter he had just had.

'Went in,' he gasped, 'and began to demand a subscription for that Nurse Fund. He'd stuck his hands in his pockets as I came in, and he sat down in his chair. Sniffed. I told him I'd heard he took an interest in scientific things. He said yes.

Sniffed again. Kept on sniffing all the time. I developed the nurse idea, and all the while kept my eyes open. Bottles—chemicals—everywhere. Test tubes in stands, and a smell of evening primrose. Would he subscribe? Said he'd consider it. Asked him, point blank, was he researching. Said he was. A long research? Got quite cross. "A damnable long research," said he, blowing the cork out, so to speak. "Oh," said I. And out came the grievance. The man was just on the boil, and my question boiled him over. He had been given a prescription, most valuable prescription—what for he wouldn't say. Was it medical?"Damn you! What are you fishing after?"

'I apologized. Dignified sniff and cough. He resumed. He'd read it. Five ingredients. Put

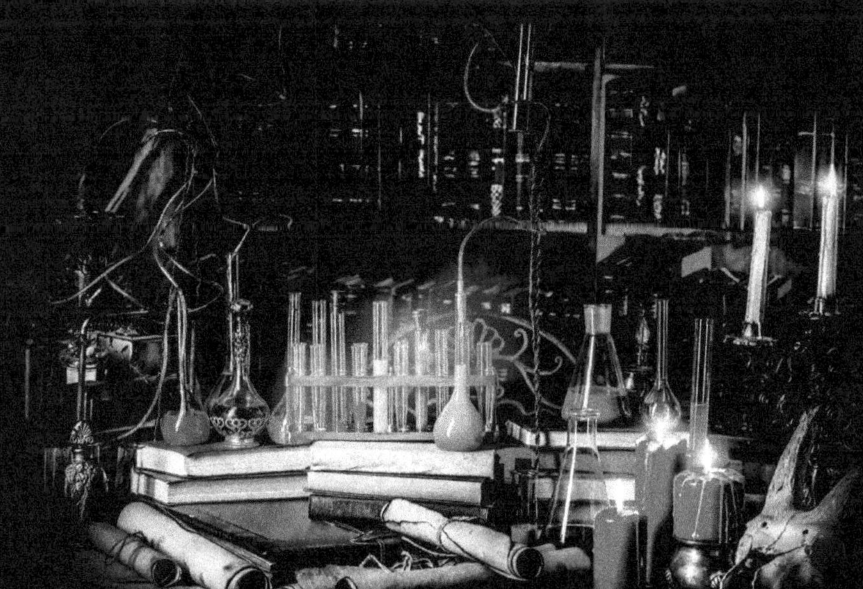

it down; turned his head. Draught of air from window lifted the paper. Swish, rustle. He was working in a room with an open fireplace, he said. Just at that point, to illustrate his story, out came his arm.'

'Well?'

'No hand—just an empty sleeve. Lord! I thought, that's a deformity!'

'Then, I thought, there's something odd in that. What the devil keeps that sleeve up and open, if there's nothing in it? There was nothing in it, I tell you.

"How the devil," said I, "can you move an empty sleeve like that?"

"It's an empty sleeve, is it? You saw it was an empty sleeve?"

'He stood up right away and came towards me in three very slow steps. Then very quietly he pulled his sleeve out of his pocket again, and raised his arm towards me.'

'Well?'

'Something—exactly like a finger and thumb it felt—nipped my nose.'

Bunting began to laugh.

Cuss turned round in a helpless way and took a second glass of the drink.

'There wasn't anything there!' said Cuss, his voice running up into a shriek. 'It's all very well for you to laugh, but I tell you I was so startled, I hit his cuff hard and turned around, and cut out of the room—I left him.

Cuss stopped. There was no mistaking the sincerity of his panic.

'When I hit his cuff,' said Cuss, 'I tell you, it felt exactly like hitting an arm. And there wasn't an arm! There wasn't the ghost of an arm!'

Mr Bunting thought it over. He looked suspiciously at Cuss.

'It's a most remarkable story,' he said. He looked very wise and grave indeed.

'It's really,' said Mr Bunting with judicial emphasis, 'a most remarkable story.'

***

The facts of the burglary at the vicarage came to them chiefly through the medium of the vicar and his wife. It occurred in the small hours of Whit Monday, the day devoted in Iping to the Club festivities. Mrs Bunting, it seemed, woke up suddenly in the stillness that came before the dawn, with the strong impression that the door of their bedroom had opened and closed. She distinctly heard the sound of bare feet as if someone was walking along the passage towards the staircase.

She woke up Mr Bunting as quietly as possible.

They discovered that the candle was lit and someone took the money from the drawer. She went hastily to the doorway. Of all the strange occurrences there was a violent sneeze in the passage. They rushed out, and as they did so the kitchen door slammed.

They both heard a sound of bolts being hastily shot back.

As they opened the kitchen door he saw through the scullery that the back door was just opening.

The place was empty. They refastened the back door, examined the kitchen, pantry and scullery thoroughly, and at last went down into the cellar. There was not a soul to be found in the house, search as they would.

***

After a while, the stranger was short of money and he had a choice to either pay his dues or leave. He revealed a part of his 'invisibility' to the landlady.

He then decided to flee and soon met a tramp, Thomas Marvel, and made him his assistant. Marvel was chubby, with a cylindrical nose and a bristling beard. They return to recover three notebooks that contain records of his experiments. Marvel betrayed him to the police, but the stranger chased him to Port Burdock, threatening to kill him. Marvel is saved by the local people in an inn, and taking this opportunity he reported about the invisible man.

When the stranger attempted to take revenge he got shot. He took shelter in Dr Kemp's house. whom he knew from medical school, and to whom he revealed his identity, and his plans to establish a reign of terror based on his discovery of invisibility. The Invisible Man was Griffin, who left medicine to study optics. He then goes on to tell Kemp of the story of how he became invisible.

'It was last December. I had taken a room in London, a large unfurnished room in a big ill-managed lodging house in a slum near Great Portland Street. The room was soon full of the appliances I had bought with my father's money; the work was going on steadily, successfully, drawing near an end. I was like a man emerging from a thicket, and suddenly coming on some unmeaning tragedy. I went to bury my father.

'I remember walking back to the empty house, through the place that had once been a village. Every way the roads ran out at last into the desecrated fields and ended in rubble heaps and rank wet weeds. I remember myself as a gaunt black figure, going along the slippery, shiny pavement and the strange sense of detachment.

'But going along the High Street, my old life came back to me for a space, for I met the girl I had known ten years since. Our eyes met.

'Something moved me to turn back and talk to her. She was a very ordinary person.

'It was all like a dream, that visit to the old places. I did not feel then that I was lonely, that I had come out from the world into a desolate place. I appreciated my loss of sympathy, but I put it down to the general inanity of things. Re-entering my room seemed like the recovery of reality. There were the things I knew and loved. There stood the apparatus, the experiments arranged and waiting. And now there was scarcely a difficulty left, beyond the planning of details.

'I will tell you, Kemp, sooner or later, all the complicated processes. We need not go into that now. For the most part, saving certain gaps I chose to remember, they are written in cypher in those books that tramp has hidden. We must hunt him down. We must get those books again. But the essential phase was to place the transparent object whose refractive index was to be lowered between two radiating centres of a sort of ethereal vibration, of which I will tell you more fully later. I needed two little dynamos, and these I worked with a cheap gas engine. My first experiment was with a bit of white wool fabric. It was the strangest thing in the world to see it in the flicker of the flashes soft and white, and then to watch it fade like a wreath of smoke and vanish.

'I could scarcely believe I had done it. I put my hand into the emptiness, and there was the thing as solid as ever. I felt it awkwardly, and threw it on the floor. I had a little trouble finding it again.

'And then came a curious experience. I heard a miaow behind me, and turning, saw a lean white cat, very dirty, outside the window. A thought came into my head. "Everything ready for you," I said, and went to the window, opened it, and called softly. She came in, purring—the poor beast was starving—and I gave her some milk. All my food was in a cupboard in the corner of the room. After that she went smelling round the room, evidently with the idea of making herself at home. The invisible rag upset her a bit; you should have seen her spit at it! But I made her comfortable on the the pillow of my truckle-bed.'

'And you processed her?'

'I processed her. But giving drugs to a cat is no joke, Kemp! And the process failed.'

'Failed!'

'In two particulars. These were the claws and the pigment stuff, what is it?—at the back of the eye in a cat. You know?'

'Tapetum.'

'Yes, the tapetum. It didn't go. After I'd given the stuff to bleach the blood and done certain other things to her, I gave the beast opium, and put her and the pillow she was sleeping on, on the apparatus. And after all the rest had faded and vanished, there remained two little ghosts of her eyes.'

'Odd!'

'I can't explain it. She was bandaged and clamped, of course—so I had her safe, but she woke while she was still misty, and miaowed dismally, and someone came knocking. It was an old woman from downstairs, who suspected me of vivisecting—a drink-sodden old creature, with only a white cat to care for in all the world. I whipped out some chloroform, applied it and answered the door. "Did I hear a cat?" she asked. "My cat?" "Not here," said I, very politely. She was a little doubtful and tried to peer past me into the room; strange enough to her no doubt—bare walls, uncurtained windows, truckle-bed, with the gas engine vibrating, and that faint ghastly stinging of chloroform in the air. She had to be satisfied at last and went away again."

'How long did it take?' asked Kemp.

'Three or four hours—the cat. The bones and sinews and the fat were the last to go, and the tips of the coloured hairs. And, as I say, the back part of the eye, tough, iridescent stuff it is, wouldn't go at all.

'It was night outside long before the business was over, and nothing was to be seen but the dim eyes and the claws. I stopped the gas engine, felt for and stroked the beast, which was still insensible, and then, being tired, left it sleeping on the invisible pillow and went to bed. I found it hard to sleep. I lay awake thinking weak aimless stuff, going over the experiment over and over again, or dreaming feverishly of things growing misty and vanishing about me, until everything, the ground I stood on, vanished, and so I came to that sickly falling nightmare one gets. About two, the cat began miaowing about the room. I tried to hush it by talking to it, and then I decided to turn it out. I remember the shock I had when striking a light—there were just the round eyes shining green—and nothing round them. I would have given it milk, but I hadn't any. It wouldn't be quiet, it just sat down and miaowed at the door. I tried to catch it, with an idea of putting it out of the window, but it wouldn't be caught, it vanished. Then it began miaowing in different parts of the room. At last I

opened the window and made a bustle. I suppose it went out at last. I never saw any more of it.

'Then—Heaven knows why—I fell thinking of my father's funeral again, and the dismal windy hillside, until the day had come. I found sleeping was hopeless, and, locking my door after me, wandered out into the morning streets.'

'You don't mean to say there's an invisible cat at large!' said Kemp.

'If it hasn't been killed,' said the Invisible Man. 'Why not?'

'Why not?' said Kemp. 'I didn't mean to interrupt.'

'It's very probably been killed,' said the Invisible Man. 'It was alive four days after because I saw a crowd round a place, trying to see whence the miaowing came.'

He was silent for the best part of a minute. Then he resumed abruptly:'I remember that morning before the change very vividly. I must have gone up Great Portland Street. I remember the barracks in Albany Street, and the horse soldiers coming out, and at last I found the summit of Primrose Hill. It was a sunny day in January—one of those sunny, frosty days that came before the snow this year. My weary brain tried to formulate the position, to plot out a plan of action.

'I was surprised to find, now that my prize was within my grasp, how inconclusive its attainment seemed. As a matter of fact I was worked out; the intense stress of nearly four years' continuous work left me incapable of any strength of feeling. I was apathetic, and I tried in vain to recover the enthusiasm of my first inquiries. Nothing seemed to matter. I saw pretty clearly this was a transient mood, due to overwork and want of sleep, and that either by drugs or rest it would be possible to recover my energies.

'All I could think clearly was that the thing had to be carried through; the fixed idea still ruled me. And soon, for the money I had was almost

exhausted. I looked about me at the hillside, with children playing and girls watching them, and tried to think of all the fantastic advantages an invisible man would have in the world. After a time I crawled home, took some food and a strong dose of strychnine, and went to sleep in my clothes on

my unmade bed. Strychnine is a grand tonic, Kemp, to take the flabbiness out of a man.'

'It's the devil,' said Kemp. 'I awoke vastly invigorated and rather irritable. You know?'

'I know the stuff.'

'And there was someone rapping at the door. It was my landlord with threats and enquiries, an old man in a long grey coat and greasy slippers. I had been tormenting a cat in the night, he was sure—the old woman's tongue had been busy. He insisted on knowing all about it. The laws in this country against vivisection were very severe—he might be liable. I denied the cat. Then the vibration of the little gas engine could be felt all over the house, he said. That was true, certainly. He edged round me into the room, peering about over his German-silver spectacles, and a sudden dread came into my mind that he might carry away something of my secret. I tried to keep between him and the concentrating apparatus I had arranged, and that only made him more curious. What was I doing? Why was I always alone and secretive? Was it legal? Was it dangerous? I paid nothing but the usual rent. His had always been a most respectable house—in a disreputable neighbourhood. Suddenly my temper gave way. I told him to get out. He began to protest, to jabber of his right of entry. In a moment I had him by the collar; something ripped, and he went spinning out into his own passage. I slammed and locked the door and sat down quivering.

'He made a fuss outside, which I disregarded, and after a time he went away.

'But this brought matters to a crisis. I did not know what he would do, nor even what he had the power to do. To move to fresh apartments would have meant delay; altogether I had barely twenty pounds left in the world, for the most part in a bank—and I could not afford that. Vanish! It was irresistible. Then there would be an inquiry, the sacking of my room.

'At the thought of the possibility of my work being exposed or interrupted at its very climax, I became very angry and active. I hurried out with my three books of notes, my cheque book—the tramp has them now—and directed them from the nearest Post Office to a house of call for letters and parcels in Great Portland Street. I tried to go out noiselessly. Coming in, I found my landlord going quietly upstairs; he had heard the door close, I suppose. You would have laughed to see him jump aside on the landing as I came tearing after him. He glared at me as I went by him, and I made the house quiver with the slamming of my door. I heard him come shuffling up to my floor, hesitate and go down. I set to work upon my preparations forthwith.

'It was all done that evening and night. While I was still sitting under the sickly, drowsy influence of the drugs that decolourize blood, there came a repeated knocking at the door. It ceased, footsteps went away and returned, and the knocking was resumed. There was an attempt to push something under the door—a blue paper. Then in a fit of irritation I rose and went and flung the door wide open.'

'It was my landlord, with a notice of ejectment or something. He held it out to me, saw something odd about my hands, I expect, and lifted his eyes to my face.

'For a moment he gaped. Then he gave a sort of inarticulate cry, dropped candle and writ together, and went blundering down the dark passage to the stairs. I shut the door, locked it and went to the looking-glass. Then I understood his terror.... My face was white—like white stone.

'But it was all horrible. I had not expected the suffering. A night of racking anguish, sickness and fainting. I set my teeth, though my skin was presently afire, all my body afire, but I lay there like grim death. I understood now how it was the cat had howled until I chloroformed it. Luckily I lived alone in my room. There were times when I sobbed and groaned and talked. But I stuck to it.... I became insensible and woke languid in the darkness.

'The pain had passed. I thought I was killing myself and I did not care. I shall never forget that dawn, and the strange horror of seeing that my hands had become as clouded glass, and watching them grow clearer and thinner as the day went by, until at last I could see the sickly disorder of my room through them, though I closed my transparent eyelids. My limbs became glassy, the bones and arteries faded, vanished, and the little white nerves went last. I gritted my teeth and stayed there to the end. At last only the dead tips of the fingernails remained, pallid and white, and the brown stain of some acid upon my fingers.

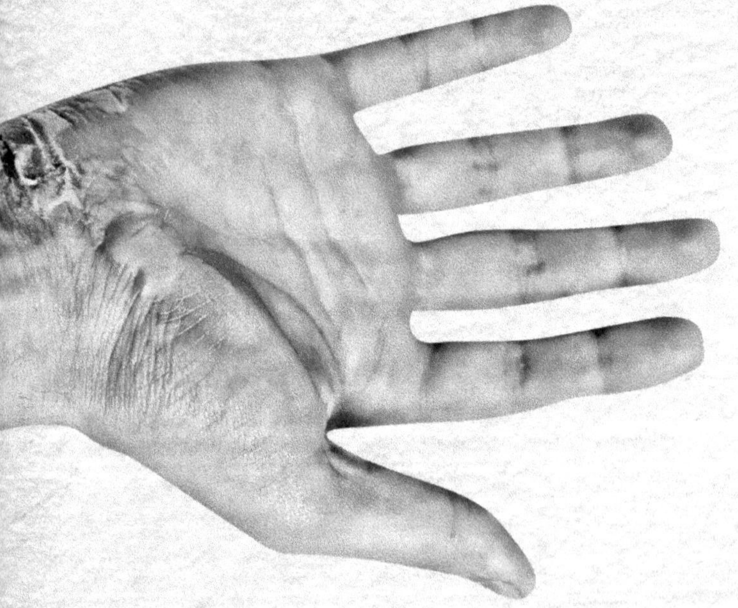

'I struggled up. At first I was as incapable as a swathed infant—stepping with limbs I could not see. I was weak and very hungry. I went and stared at nothing in my shaving-glass, at nothing save where an attenuated pigment still remained behind the retina of my eyes, fainter than mist. I had to hang on to the table and press my forehead against the glass.

'It was only by a frantic effort of will that I dragged myself back to the apparatus and completed the process.

'I slept during the forenoon, pulling the sheet over my eyes to shut out the light, and about midday I was awakened again by a knocking. My strength had returned. I sat up and listened and heard a whispering. I sprang to my feet and as noiselessly as possible began to detach the connections of my apparatus, and to distribute it about the room, so as to destroy the suggestions of its arrangement. Presently the knocking was renewed and voices called, first my landlord's, and then two others. To gain time I answered them. The invisible rag and pillow came to hand and I opened the window and pitched them out on to the cistern cover. As the window opened, a heavy crash came at the door. Someone had charged it with the idea of smashing the lock. But the stout bolts I had screwed up some days before stopped him. That startled me, made me angry. I began to tremble and do things hurriedly.

'I tossed together some loose paper, straw, packing paper, and so forth, in the middle of the room, and turned on the gas. Heavy blows began to rain upon the door. I could not find the matches. I beat my hands on the wall with rage. I turned down the gas again, stepped out of the window on the cistern cover, very softly lowered the sash, and sat down, secure and invisible, but quivering with anger, to watch events. They split a panel, I saw, and in another moment they had broken away the staples of the bolts and stood in the open doorway. It was the landlord and his two stepsons, sturdy young men in their twenties. Behind them fluttered the old hag of a woman from downstairs.

'You may imagine their astonishment to find the room empty. One of the younger men rushed to the window at once, flung it up and stared out. His staring eyes and thick-lipped bearded face came a foot from my face. I was half-minded to hit his silly face, but I arrested my doubled fist. He stared right

through me. So did the others as they joined him. The old man went and peered under the bed, and then they all made a rush for the cupboard. They had to argue about it at length. They concluded I had not answered them, that their imagination had deceived them. A feeling of extraordinary joy took the place of my anger as I sat outside the window and watched these four people—for the old lady came in, glancing suspiciously about her like a cat, trying to understand the riddle of my behaviour.

'The old man agreed with the old lady that I was a vivisectionist. The sons protested in garbled English that I was an electrician, and pointed to the dynamos and radiators. They were all nervous about my arrival, although I found subsequently that they had bolted the front door. The old lady peered into the cupboard and under the bed, and one of the young men pushed up the register and stared up the chimney.

'It occurred to me that the radiators, if they fell into the hands of some acute well-educated person, would give me away too much, and watching my opportunity, I came into the room and tilted one of the little dynamos off its fellow on which it was standing, and smashed both apparatus. Then, while they were trying to explain the smash, I dodged out of the room and went softly downstairs.

'I went into one of the sitting rooms and

waited until they came down, still speculating and argumentative, all a little disappointed at finding no "horrors", and all a little puzzled how they stood legally towards me. Then I slipped up again with a box of matches, fired my heap of paper and rubbish, put the chairs and bedding thereby, led the gas to the affair, by means of an india-rubber tube, and waving a farewell to the room left it for the last time.'

'You set the house on fire!' exclaimed Kemp.

'Yes. It was the only way to cover my trail—and no doubt it was insured. I slipped the bolts of the front door quietly and went out into the street. I was invisible, and I was only just beginning to realize the extraordinary advantage my invisibility gave me. My head was already teeming with plans of all the wild and wonderful things I had now impunity to do.'

***

The Invisible Man then treated Kemp as his confidant and described his plan to begin a 'Reign of Terror' by using his invisibility to spread panic and terror the nation.

Kemp had already sent for the authorities. Summoning the police, Kemp puts his own life in jeopardy, but he survives and an exhausted, irrational Griffin is eventually subdued and killed.

DRACULA

Bram Stoker

3 May. Bistritz.— Left Munich at 8:35 p.m., on 1 May, arriving at Vienna early next morning. Buda-Pesth seems a wonderful place, from the glimpse which I got of it from the train and the little I could walk through the streets.

I feared to go very far from the station, as we had arrived late and would start as near the correct time as possible. We left in pretty good time, and came after nightfall to Klausenburgh. Here I stopped for the night at the Hotel Royale. I had for dinner, or rather supper a chicken done up some way with red pepper, which was very good. Having had some time when in London, I had visited the British Museum, and searched among the books and maps in the library regarding Transylvania; it had struck me that some knowledge of the country could be of importance in dealing with a nobleman of that country. I find that the district he named is in the extreme east

of the country, just on the borders of three states, Transylvania, Moldavia and Bukovina, in the midst of the Carpathian Mountains; one of the wildest and least-known portions of Europe. I was not able to trace Castle Dracula, but I found that Bistritz, the post town named by Count Dracula, is a fairly well-known place.

I did not sleep well, though my bed was comfortable enough, for I had all sorts of queer dreams. I had to hurry breakfast, for the train started a little before eight.

It was on the dark side of twilight when we got to Bistritz. Count Dracula had directed me to go to the Golden Krone Hotel, which I found, to my great delight, to be thoroughly old-fashioned. I was greeted by the landlady and soon her husband handed me a letter—"My Friend—Welcome to the Carpathians. I am anxiously expecting you. Sleep well tonight. At three tomorrow you will start for Bukovina; a place on it is kept for you. At the Borgo Pass my carriage will be waiting and will bring you to me. I trust that your journey from London has been a happy one, and that you will enjoy your stay in my beautiful land.

Your friend,

Dracula."

4 May—

When I asked my landlord if he knew Count Dracula, and could tell me anything of his castle, both he and his wife crossed themselves, and, saying that they knew nothing at all, simply refused

to speak further. It was all very mysterious and not by any means comforting.

Just before I was leaving, the old lady came up to my room and said in a very hysterical way, 'Must you go? Oh! Young Herr, must you go?'

When I told her that I must go at once, and that I was engaged on important business, she asked again, 'Do you know what day it is?'

I answered that it was the fourth of May. She shook her head as she said again, 'Oh, yes! I know that! I know that, but do you know what day it is?'

On my saying that I did not understand, she went on, 'It is the eve of St George's Day. Do you not know that tonight, when the clock strikes midnight, all the evil things in the world will have full sway? Do you know where you are going, and what you are going to?'

Finally she went down on her knees and pleaded not to go; at least to wait a day or two before starting. She then rose and dried her eyes, and taking a crucifix from her neck offered it to me.

She said, 'For your mother's sake', and went out of the room.

I am writing up this part of the diary whilst I am waiting for the coach, which is, of course, late; and the crucifix is still round my neck. Whether it is the old lady's fear, or the many ghostly traditions of this place, or the crucifix itself, I do not know, but I am not feeling nearly as easy in my mind as usual. Here comes the coach!

5 May,the Castle— When I got on the coach the driver had not taken his seat, and I saw him talking with the landlady. They were evidently talking about me, for every now and then they looked at me. When we started, the crowd round the inn door, which had by this time swelled to a considerable size, all made the sign of the cross and pointed two fingers towards me. With some difficulty I got a fellow-passenger to tell me what they meant; he explained that it was a charm or guard against the evil eye.

I soon lost sight and recollection of ghostly fears in the beauty of the scene as we drove along. As we wound on our endless way, and the sun sank lower and lower behind us, the shadows of the evening began to creep round us. We kept on ascending, with occasional periods of quick descent, but in the main always ascending. Suddenly, I became conscious of the fact that the

driver was in the act of pulling up the horses in the courtyard of a vast ruined castle, from whose tall black windows came no ray of light. When the carriage stopped, the driver jumped down and held out his hand to assist me to alight. As I stood, the driver jumped again into his seat and shook the reins; the horses started forward, and trap and all disappeared down one of the dark openings.

I happened to glance at the castle which was very grim. It was looking like a horror castle, there was darkness all around. I felt imprisoned in doubts and fear. What sort of place had I come to, and among what kind of people? What sort of grim adventure was it on which I had embarked? Was this a customary incident in the life of a solicitor's clerk sent out to explain the purchase of a London estate to a foreigner? Solicitor's clerk! My fiancée Mina would not like that. Solicitor—for just before leaving London I got a word that my examination was successful, and I am now a full-blown solicitor!

All I could do now was to be patient, and to wait the coming of the morning. Just as I had come to this conclusion I heard a heavy step approaching behind the great door. A key was turned with the loud grating noise and the great door swung back. Within, stood a tall, old man with a long, white moustache, dressed in black. He held in his hand an antique silver lamp, in which the flame burned without a chimney.

'Welcome to my house! Enter freely and of your own will!' He made no motion of stepping to meet me, but stood like a statue. The instant, however, that I had stepped over the threshold, he moved impulsively forward, and holding out his hand grasped mine with a strength which made me wince, an effect which was not lessened by the fact that it seemed as cold as ice—more like the hand of a dead than a living man. Again he said, 'Welcome to my house. Come freely. Go safely; and leave something of the happiness you bring!'

I asked,' Count Dracula?'

He bowed in a courtly way as he replied, 'I am Dracula, and I bid you welcome, Mr Jonathan Harker, to my house. Come in; you must need to eat and rest.'

He took me to the bedroom and asked me to wash for supper. I was relieved of all my fears by Count Dracula's warm greeting. When, I got refreshed, I went to the other room. I found supper already laid out. I took my seat and handed to him the sealed letter which Mr Hawkins had entrusted to me. He opened it and read it gravely. Then, with a charming smile, he handed it to me to read. One passage of it, at least, gave me an excitement of pleasure.

I must regret that an attack of gout, from which malady I am a constant sufferer, forbids absolutely any travelling on my part for some time to come. But I am happy to say I can send a sufficient substitute, one in whom I have every possible confidence. He is a young man, full of energy and talent in his own way, and of a very faithful disposition. He is discreet and silent, and has grown into manhood in my service. He shall be ready to attend on you when you will during his stay, and shall take your instructions in all matters.

By this time I had finished my supper, and by my host's had drawn up a chair by the fire and began to smoke a cigar. I had now an opportunity of observing him.

His face was strongly built with a very strong aquiline, high bridge of the thin nose, peculiarly arched nostrils, lofty domed forehead and hair growing scantily round the temples but profusely elsewhere. His eyebrows were huge, almost meeting over the nose, and with bushy hair that seemed to curl in its own profusion.

The mouth, so far as I could see it under the heavy moustache, was fixed and rather cruel-looking, with peculiarly sharp white teeth. These protruded over the lips, whose remarkable rudeness showed astonishing vitality in a man of his years. For the rest, his ears were pale, and at the tops extremely pointed. The chin was broad and strong, and the cheeks firm but thin.

I had also noticed the back of his hands as they lay on his knees in the firelight, and they appeared rather white and fine. But seeing them now close to me, I could not but notice that they were rather coarse, broad, with squat fingers. It was strange to say that there were hairs in the centre of the palm. The nails were long and fine, and cut to a sharp point.

As the Count leaned over me and his hands touched me, I could not repress a shudder. It may have been that his breath was rank, but a horrible feeling of sickness came over me. He asked me to take rest. Then I went to my bedroom.

7 May — It is again early morning, but I have rested and enjoyed the last twenty-four hours. When I had dressed myself I went into the room where we had supped, and found a cold breakfast laid out with hot coffee. There was a card on the table, on which was written: 'I have to be absent for a while. Do not wait for me.—D.' I set it aside and enjoyed a hearty meal.

I noticed that there were no servants or mirrors. I looked about for something to read, for I did not like to go about the castle until I had asked the Count's permission. There was absolutely

nothing in the room, book, newspaper, or even writing materials; so I opened another door in the room and found a sort of library with a vast number of English books. Soon after Dracula entered the room and we talked about business and the purchase of Dracula's estate in England. He told me to go anywhere I wished in the castle except where the doors were locked.

'We are in Transylvania, and Transylvania is not England. Our ways are not your ways, and there shall be to you many strange things.'

After Dracula left the room, I found an atlas, in which I observed the map of England. On looking

at it, I found in certain places little rings marked, and on examining these I noticed that one was near London on the east side, manifestly where his new estate was situated; the other two were Exeter, and Whitby on the Yorkshire coast.

8 May — I only slept a few hours when I went to bed, and feeling that I could not sleep any more, got up. It was a strange fear I was experiencing. I had hung my shaving glass by the window, and was just beginning to shave. Suddenly I felt a hand on my shoulder, and heard the Count's voice saying to me, 'Good morning.' I started, for it amazed me that I had not seen him, since the reflection of the glass covered the whole room behind me. In starting I had cut myself slightly. The Count made a grab at my throat, but the crucifix around my neck thwarted him.

Dracula said, 'Take care, take care how you cut yourself. It is more dangerous than you think in this country.'

Then seizing the shaving glass, he went on, 'And this is the wretched thing that has done the mischief. It is a foul bauble of man's vanity. Away with it!'

And opening the heavy window with one hand, he flung out the glass, which was shattered into a thousand pieces on the stones of the courtyard far below, and left. When I went into the dining room, breakfast was prepared, but I could not find the Count anywhere. So I breakfasted alone. It is strange that as yet I have not seen the Count eat or drink. After breakfast I did a little exploring in the castle, and found a room looking towards the South. The castle was on the very edge of a precipice. A stone falling from the window would fall a thousand feet without touching anything! As far as the eye can reach there was a sea of green tree tops, with occasionally a deep rift where there was a chasm. Here and there were silver threads where the rivers wound in deep gorges through the forests.

I explored further; doors everywhere, and all locked and bolted. In no place save from the windows is there an available exit. The castle is a veritable prison, and I am a prisoner!

***

The more Harker investigates the nature of his confinement, the more uneasy he becomes. He realizes that the Count possesses supernatural powers and diabolical ambitions. One evening, Harker is nearly attacked by three beautiful and seductive female vampires, but the Count staves

them off, telling the vampires that Harker belongs to him. Fearing for his life, Harker attempts to escape from the castle by climbing down the walls.

***

In a few days the Russian ship, *Demeter*, after deploying cargo at Varna, ran aground on the shores of Whitby.

Log of the *Demeter*

Varna to Whitby

13 July—Crew dissatisfied about something. Seemed scared, but would not speak out.

14 July—I was somewhat anxious about crew. A Mate could not make out what was wrong; they only told him there was *something*, and crossed themselves. Mate lost temper with one of them that day and struck him. Expected fierce quarrel, but all was quiet.

16 July—A mate reported in the morning that one of the crew members was missing.

17 July—Yesterday, one of the men came to my cabin, and in an awestruck way confided to me that he thought there was a strange man aboard the ship.

24 July—Last night, another man lost, disappeared. Like the first, he came off his watch and was not seen again. All men were in a panic of fear.

29 July—When the morning watch came on deck could find no one except steersman. Raised outcry, and all came on deck. Thorough search, but no one found.

2 August, midnight—Woke up from few minutes sleep by hearing a cry, seemingly outside my port. When I saw there was not a sign of man.

4 August—My friend jumped overboard to escape the monster and I was left alone. I felt guilty. I blamed myself, who killed all the sailors. I was the captain, and I must not leave my ship. But I should confuse this monster, for I should tie my hands to the wheel when my strength began to fail.

No trace has ever been found of the great dog; at which there is much mourning, for, with public opinion in its present state, he would, I believe, be adopted by the town.

Mina's Journal

My friend, Lucy Westenra has received marriage proposals from Dr John Seward, Quincey

Morris and the Hon. Arthur Holmwood (later Lord Godalming), and chose to settle down with Holmwood. I have to go and visit her at Whitby.

8 August—I saw Lucy sleepwalking. This is very concerning, and she is not telling anything. I really think that she must be feeling restless about something.

11 August, 3 a.m.—Another sleepless night. Lucy was sleepwalking again. I woke up to realized that she was not in the room. I saw her walking out of the house, and followed her to a cemetery. To my horror, I saw a figure laying her on the ground and bending over her. When I screamed, I saw the figure look at my direction with glowing red eyes, and then run away. I rushed to Lucy's side, she was breathing but was unconscious. I saw two puncture

marks on her neck and tried to wake her up, and finally come back home.

19 August — I finally heard from my dear Johnathan. He was ill and so could not write to me. I am going to Budapest to see him and maybe marry too! Lucy will take back my luggage to London with her.

From Dr Seward's Diary

7 September—I was summoned recently by Lucy's fiancé, to take a look at her as she was not keeping well. Lucy's case is quite peculiar; her symptoms are something I have never seen before, and not to mention the marks on her neck. I had written to Professor Van Helsing to request him to come and examine Lucy, and give a proper diagnosis. He was my professor and mentor in the university, and I knew the details of the case will interest him.

He did come and see Lucy. Immediately, he ordered the Lucy's room to be filled with garlic, but his face betrayed concern.

9 September—I am glad to report that Lucy's condition is improving. She is much better now.

17 September—I was engaged after dinner in my study when suddenly the door was burst open, and in rushed my patient, with a dinner knife in his hand.

He struck at me and cut my left wrist rather severely. My wrist bled freely, and quite a little pool trickled on to the carpet. The patient then began to lick the resulting blood off of the floor. As the attendants dragged him away, he was screaming, 'The blood is the life!'

Then, I received a telegram from Van Helsing, ordering me to return to Lucy. The telegram arrived twenty-two hours late. I had just caught a train to London.

18 September—I arrived to Hillingham as soon as I got the telegram, but there was no answer at the door and the house was locked. Van Helsing arrived, I explained the situation, and we entered into the house through the window. When we entered in the room we saw the drugged servants and found Lucy and her mother's body in Lucy's room.

As she was still alive—barely—we woke the servants to prepare a bath while we revived her. The servants did as instructed, and also answered the door, where a man had arrived with a telegram from Arthur. I had never seen Professor take such interest in a case before. I knew, as he knew, that it was a stand-up fight with death, and in a pause told him so. He said, 'If that were all, I would stop here where we are now, and let her fade away into peace, for I see no light in life over her horizon.'

He went on with his work with, if possible, renewed and more frenzied vigour. He concluded that Lucy would require blood transfusions. We had some volunteers, but we needed another donor who was fit enough to supply blood. The man who delivered the telegram volunteered; I immediately recognized him as my old friend, Quincey Morris. We read the telegram, which was a request for news about Lucy, and we performed yet another blood transfusion, with the American as the donor.

I began to take care of Mrs Westenra's death certificate in order to prevent an investigation that would disturb Lucy; Morris prepared a telegram for Arthur.

Morris figured out that the transfusion was not an isolated incident and demanded information. We told what Lucy had been through and he was distraught and almost broke down completely. He could not understand where the missing blood had gone, and gladly volunteered his services in any way possible.

When Lucy woke up, she grieved for her mother, then fell back asleep.

19 September— We kept a vigil during the night, and sent for Holmwood the next day. By this time, we noticed that Lucy's teeth appeared longer and sharper, and Lucy herself was in terrible condition.

Lucy got a letter from Mina. She got the news that Mina's married life was going well in Exeter.

20 September — A report from Patrick Hennesey was added about my patient Renfield, who had run away twice to the house next door crying, 'I'll fight for my lord and master.' (He suffers from delusions which compel him to eat living creatures in the hope of obtaining their life-force for himself.) In the night time when I was in Lucy's room, I noticed a large bat flying outside her window.

At six o'clock Van Helsing came to relieve me. Arthur had then fallen asleep. When he saw Lucy's face I could hear the hissing breath, and he said to me in a sharp whisper, 'Draw up the blind. I want light!'

Then he bent down, and, with his face almost touching Lucy's, examined her carefully. He removed the flowers and lifted the silk handkerchief from her throat.

He said that she was dying and asked Arthur to come to the room.

Seeing Arthur, she whispered softly, 'Arthur! Oh, my love, I am so glad you have come!'

When Arthur sat beside her, Van Helsing kept Arthur from kissing Lucy at first, claiming that holding her hand would comfort her more.

And then I noticed a strange change in her. She opened her eyes, which were now dull and hard at once, and said in a soft voice, she said, 'Arthur! Oh, my love, I am so glad you have come!'

Arthur bent eagerly over to kiss her, but at that instant Van Helsing, who, like me, had been startled by her voice, swooped upon him, and catching him by the neck with both hands, dragged him back with a fury of strength which I never thought he could have possessed, and actually hurled Arthur almost across the room.

'Not on your life!' he said. 'Not for your living soul and hers!'

Arthur was so taken aback that he did not for a moment know what to do or say, and before any impulse of violence could seize him he realized the place and the occasion, and stood silent, waiting.

I kept my eyes fixed on Lucy, as did Van Helsing, and we saw a spasm as of rage flit like a shadow over her face. The sharp teeth clamped together. Then her eyes closed, and she breathed heavily and died. When I reflected that she had finally met her peaceful end, Van Helsing corrected me. 'Not so! Alas! Not so. It was only the beginning!'

The funeral was held the next day. On the day after that, Arthur had to return to his own estate to bury his father, who just died. Van Helsing insisted on dealing with Lucy's papers.

Van Helsing, Arthur and I, as well as the funeral director, all felt that Lucy looked disturbingly lifelike in death.

Van Helsing placed garlic in the coffin and a golden crucifix on her mouth. He then quietly recruited me to help him cut off Lucy's head and take out her heart. I promised to follow his wishes, no matter how strange. However, he told me later that it was not necessary to disturb her yet, as someone removed the crucifix from her mouth. I was left confused.

Mrs Westenra's solicitor informed me and Van Helsing that the entire estate was left to Arthur, who, through the unfortunate loss of his father and his lover, was now Lord Godalming, master of two estates. Arthur told me that he loved Lucy very much and thanked me for all his help, then broke down. Van Helsing asked Arthur for the right to control Lucy's papers for the time being. Arthur gladly granted him that right. Van Helsing told us that we had a difficult journey ahead of ourselves but must be brave and unselfish.

Following Lucy's death, press reports cited children being stalked and haunted in the night by a beautiful lady. Van Helsing, learnt that Lucy had become a vampire. He shared the development with Seward, Lord Godalming and Morris after which they helped him track her down and, after confronting her, staked her heart, beheaded her and filled her mouth with garlic.

Johnathan Harker's Journal

26 September—I arrived from Budapest, where Mina and I were married. We too joined Helsing and the suitors against Dracula. My dear Mina is helping Professor Helsing find more information about Dracula.

Dr Seward's Journal

3 October—Through various hits and misses, we have been able to track down the location of Dracula. Once, Van Helsing figured out that we needed to track the boxes from the cursed Russian ship, the rest was relatively easy. But we did not anticipate what happened later. Renfield, was becoming more and more restless, and kept screaming for his master. I had questioned him about the master, on Helsings's insistence, but didn't get any substantial information.

Dracula learnt of Van Helsing's coalition against him. He made Renfield help him get to Mina. He attacked Mina thrice, and fed her with his own

blood to gain control over her.

Van Helsing told Jonathan to stay and protect Mina while the others were asked to go to find the ship that carried Dracula. Van Helsing realized that Dracula knew that he was beaten in London, and so loaded his last box onto a ship.

Mina Harker's Journal

5 October, 5 p.m.— Van Helsing, Lord Godalming, Dr Seward, Mr Quincey Morris, Jonathan Harker and I met to discuss the plan to catch Dracula. Arthur discovered which boat was bound for the Black Sea. The men spoke with the dockworkers and found that a man fitting Dracula's description managed to get himself a place on the boat, which was leaving before the turn of the tide.

Dracula called in a fog to keep the boat docked until after the tide turned, so that he could board it. We found out who was receiving the box, and how long it will take to get there.

Dr Seward's Diary

5 October– Van Helsing and I noticed that Mina was changing like Lucy changed. We realized that Dracula might be able to find out what we were doing by reading Mina's thoughts. We resolved to keep her uninformed once again.

Later—At the very outset of our meeting a great relief was experienced by both Van Helsing and myself. Mrs Harker had sent a message by her husband to say that she would not join us at present, as she thought it better that we should be free to discuss our movements without her presence to embarrass us. For my own part, I thought that if Mrs Harker realized the danger herself, it was much pain as well as much danger averted. Keeping in mind that we needed to reach Dracula's castle before him, we devised a plan.

Van Helsing said, 'And as I think that Varna [a seaport on the Black Sea] is not familiar to any of us, why not go there soon? It is as long to wait here as there. Tonight and tomorrow we can get ready, and then if all be well, we four can set out on our journey.'

'We four?' asked Harker.

'Of course!' answered the Professor quickly. 'You must remain to take care of your so sweet wife!'

Harker was silent for a while and then said in a hollow voice, 'Let us talk of that part of it in the morning. I want to consult with Mina.'

I thought that now was the time for Van Helsing to warn him not to disclose our plan to her, but he took no notice. I looked at him significantly and coughed. For answer he put his finger to his lips and turned away.

Jonathan Harker's Journal

5 October — Mina insisted that I tell her nothing of our plans, and I agreed, even though it made me uncomfortable. However, she insisted that she went with us on our journey because if Dracula called for her, she would go alone, without the safety of the group, and would use every possible way to reach his goal. We agreed with her logic, so she came along.

We formed a plan to put a branch of wild rose on the box when we found him, then to kill him when we had the chance, even if it means in the presence of onlookers. Van Helsing warned us that plans have a way of changing.

11 October— I asked Dr Seward to check Mina's health. She begged him to destroy her if by chance she changed totally. Filled with emotion, yet touched by her bravery, the men agreed.

15 October, Varna — We left Charring Cross on the 12th, got to Paris in the night, boarded the *Orient Express* and reached Varna. Mina was hypnotized. Dracula was still on the sea. We were preparing all our weapons especially I was sharpening my kukri knife. Dracula's ship was late. We sat down discussing his psyche.

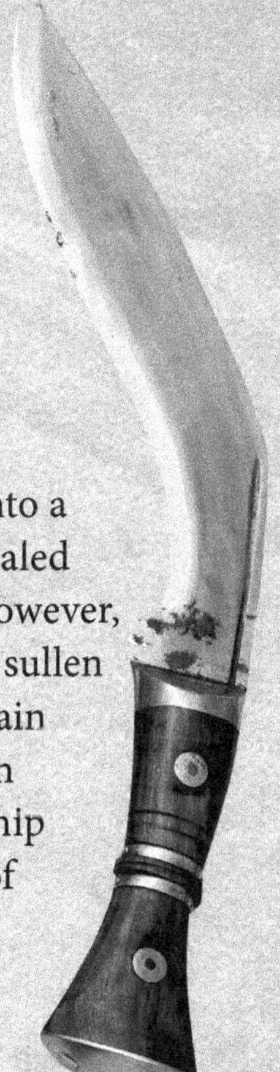

Dr Seward's Diary

29 October— Mina went into a hypnotic trance again and revealed that the Count had reached. However, he was changing so he became sullen and refused to speak. The captain of the ship revealed to Jonathan that there was trouble on the ship because of the boxes. A letter of instructions had been sent to the businessman Emmanuel Hildesheim to clear and take away the boxes before sunrise,

which was to be collected by Petrof Skinsky, an agent of Dracula. But the men had lost the trail of Skinsky. Mina surmised that the Count had decided to return to his castle by water through a secret way. He had also murdered Skinsky. To erase the trail, we all planned to meet by separate ways in Transylvania at Dracula's castle.

Mina Harker's Journal

1 November—Van Helsing was worried about me because not only I could be hypnotized but also because I was becoming healthier and redder. So, after reaching the castle, Van Helsing made a ring around me and put some holy water on it. Suddenly, from the mist the three women that Jonathan had seen in the castle tried to entice me, but they could not come in because of the holy ring. Inside an old chapel, Van Helsing found three graves and he found the three beautiful women who were vampires. He severed their heads. Suddenly, Van Helsing saw a band of gypsies carrying a carriage with a big chest, which he surmised, was Dracula's coffin. He saw two horsemen, Quincey and John following them, and on the other side they saw Jonathan and Arthur following. A battle ensued between the gypsies and them. Jonathan rushed up to the chest with Quincey Morris and plunged the knife into the heart of Dracula and Dracula died. But Quincey

was wounded and cried, 'Now God be thanked that all has not been in vain', and died.

Note

Seven years later, a son was born to us on the death anniversary of Quincey, whom we called Quincey. We burned the rest of all the evidence, as we believed no one would believe us and story of Count Dracula. We lived happily ever after.

Johnathan Harker

Other Titles *in the* Series

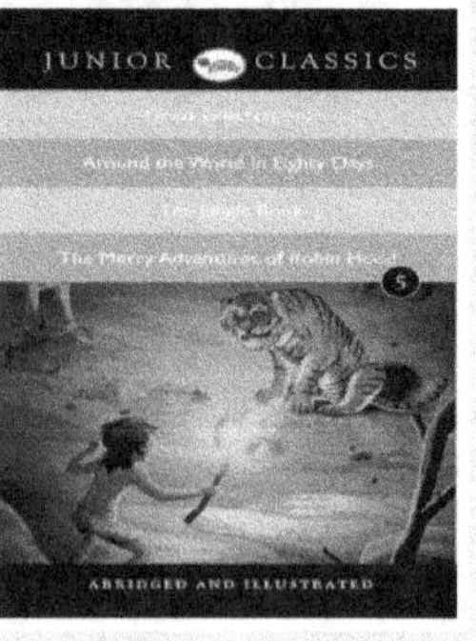

www.ingramcontent.com/pod-product-compliance
Lightning Source LLC
LaVergne TN
LVHW010839120826
845149LV00017B/3314